Roger Brooke Taney

Habeas Corpus

The Proceedings in the Case of John Merryman, of Baltimore County,

Maryland, before the Hon. Roger Brooke Taney, Chief Justice of the

Supreme Court of the United States

Roger Brooke Taney

Habeas Corpus
The Proceedings in the Case of John Merryman, of Baltimore County, Maryland, before the Hon. Roger Brooke Taney, Chief Justice of the Supreme Court of the United States

ISBN/EAN: 9783337398385

Printed in Europe, USA, Canada, Australia, Japan

Cover: Foto ©Andreas Hilbeck / pixelio.de

More available books at **www.hansebooks.com**

HABEAS CORPUS.

THE PROCEEDINGS

IN THE CASE OF

JOHN MERRYMAN,

OF

BALTIMORE COUNTY, MARYLAND,

BEFORE THE

HON. ROGER BROOKE TANEY,

CHIEF JUSTICE of the SUPREME COURT of the UNITED STATES.

BALTIMORE:

PUBLISHED BY LUCAS BROTHERS, 170 BALTIMORE-ST.

1861.

STATEMENT OF THE CASE.

On the 26th May, A. D. 1861, the following sworn petition was presented to the Chief Justice of the United States on behalf of John Merryman, he being at the time in confinement in Fort McHenry.

To the HON. ROGER B. TANEY,

Chief Justice of the Supreme Court of the U. States.

The petition of John Merryman, of Baltimore county, and State of Maryland, respectfully shows, that being at home, in his own domicil, he was, about the hour of 2 o'clock, A. M., on the 25th of May, A. D. 1861, aroused from his bed by an armed force pretending to act under military orders from some person to your petitioner unknown. That he was by said armed force, deprived of his liberty by being taken into custody, and removed from his said home to Fort McHenry, near to the city of Baltimore, and in the district aforesaid, and where your petitioner now is in close custody.

That he has been so imprisoned without any process or color of law whatsoever, and that none such is pretended by those who are thus detaining him; and that no warrant from any court, magistrate, or other person having legal authority to issue the same exists to justify such arrest; but, to the contrary, the same, as above stated, hath been done without color of law, and in violation of the Constitution and laws of the United States, of which he is a citizen. That since his arrest he has been informed that some order purporting to come from one General Keim, of Pennsylvania, to this petitioner unknown, directing the arrest of the Captain of some company in Baltimore county, of which company the petitioner never was and is not captain, was the pretended ground of his arrest, and is the sole ground, as he believes, on which he is now detained.

That the person now so detaining him at said Fort is Brigadier General George Cadwalader, the military commander of said post, professing to act in the premises under or by color of the authority of the United States. Your petitioner therefore prays that the writ of habeas corpus may issue, to be directed to the said George Cadwalader, commanding him to produce your petitioner before you, Judge as aforesaid, with the cause, if any, for his arrest and detention, to the end that your petitioner be discharged and restored to liberty, and as in duty, &c.

JOHN MERRYMAN.

Fort McHenry, 25th May, 1861.

United States of America, District of Maryland, to wit:

Before the subscriber, a Commissioner appointed by the Circuit Court of the United States, in and for the fourth circuit and district of Maryland, to take affidavits, &c., personally appeared the 25th day of May, A. D. 1861, Geo. H. Williams, of the city of Baltimore and district aforesaid, and made oath on the Holy Evangely of Almighty God that the matters and facts stated in the foregoing petition are true, to the best of his knowledge, information and belief, and that the said petition was signed in his presence by the petitioner, and would have been sworn to by him, said petitioner, but that he was at the time and still is in close custody, and all access to him denied, except to his counsel and his brother-in-law—this deponent being one of said counsel.

Sworn to before me, this 25th day of May, A. D. 1861.

JOHN HANAN, *U. S. Commissioner.*

United States of America, District of Maryland, to wit:

Before the subscriber, a Commissioner appointed by the Circuit Court of the United States, in and for the fourth circuit and district of Maryland, to take affidavits, &c., personally appeared this 26th day of May, 1861, George H. Williams, of the city of Baltimore and district aforesaid, and made oath on the Holy Evangely of Almighty God that on the 26th day of May he went to Fort McHenry, in the preceding affidavit mentioned, and obtained an interview with Gen. Geo. Cadwalader, then and there in command, and deponent, one of the counsel of said John Merryman, in the foregoing petition named, and at his request, and declaring himself to be such counsel, requested and demanded that he might be permitted to see the written papers, and to be permitted to make copies thereof, under and by which he, the said General, detained the said Merryman in custody, and that to said demand the said Gen. Cadwalader replied that he would neither permit the deponent, though officially requesting and demanding, as such counsel, to read the said papers, nor to have or make copies thereof.

Sworn to this 26th day of May, A. D. 1861, before me.

JOHN HANAN,

U. S. Commissioner for Maryland.

Upon this petition the Chief Justice passed the following order:

In the matter of the petition of John Merryman, for a writ of habeas corpus:

Ordered, this 26th day of May, A. D. 1861, that the writ of habeas corpus issue in this case, as prayed, and that the same be directed to General George Cadwalader, and be issued in the usual form, by Thomas Spicer, clerk of the Circuit Court of the United States in and for the district of Maryland, and that the said writ of habeas corpus be returnable at eleven o'clock, on Monday, the 27th of May, 1861, at the Circuit Court room, in the Masonic Hall, in the city of Baltimore, before me, Chief Justice of the Supreme Court of the United States.

R. B. TANEY.

In obedience to this order, Mr. Spicer issued the following writ:

District of Maryland, to wit: the United States of America:

To GENERAL GEORGE CADWALADER, *Greeting:*

You are hereby commanded to be and appear before the Honorable ROGER B. TANEY, Chief Justice of the Supreme Court of the United States, at the United States Court Room, in the Masonic Hall, in the city of Baltimore, on Monday, the 27th day of May, 1861, at 11 o'clock in the morning, and that you have with you the body of John Merryman, of Baltimore county, and now in your custody, and that you certify and make known the day and cause of the caption and detention of the said John Merryman, and that you then and there do submit it to, and receive whatsoever the said Chief Justice shall determine upon concerning you on this behalf, according to law, and have you then and there this writ.

Witness, the Honorable R. B. TANEY, Chief Justice of our Supreme Court, &c., &c., &c.

THOS. SPICER, Clerk.

Issued 26th May, 1861.

The Marshal made his return that he had served the writ on General Cadwalader on the same day on which it issued, and filed that return on the 27th May, 1861, on which day at 11 o'clock precisely the Chief Justice took his seat on the Bench. In a few minutes Colonel Lee, a military officer, appeared with General Cadwalader's return to the writ, which is as follows:

HEADQUARTERS, DEPARTMENT OF ANNAPOLIS,

Fort McHenry, May 26, 1861.

To the HON. ROGER B. TANEY,

Chief Justice of the Supreme Court of the United States, Baltimore, Md.

Sir—The undersigned, to whom the annexed writ of this date, signed by Thomas Spicer, clerk of the Supreme Court of the United States, is directed, most respectfully states, that the arrest of Mr. John Merryman, in the said writ named, was not made with his knowledge or by his order or direction, but was made by Col. Samuel Yohe, acting under the orders of Major General Wm. H. Keim, both of said officers, being in the military service of the United States, but not within the limits of his command.

The prisoner was brought to this post on the 20th inst. by Adjutant James Wittimore and Lieut. Wm. H. Abel, by order of Col. Yohe, and is charged with various acts of treason, and with being publicly associated with and holding a commission as lieutenant in a company having in their possession arms belonging to the United States, and avowing his purpose of armed hostility against the government. He is also informed that it can be clearly established that the prisoner has made often and unreserved declarations of his association with this organized force as being in avowed hostility to the government, and in readiness to co-operate with those engaged in the present rebellion against the government of the United States. He has further to inform you that he is duly authorized by the President of the United States in such cases to suspend the writ of habeas corpus for the public safety.

This is a high and delicate trust, and it has been enjoined upon him that it should be executed with judgment and discretion, but he is nevertheless also instructed that in times of civil strife, errors, if any, should be on the side of the safety of the country. He most respectfully submits for your consideration that those who should co-operate in the present trying and painful position in which our country is placed, should not, by any unnecessary want of confidence in each other, increase our embarrassments.

He therefore respectfully requests that you will postpone further action upon this case until he can receive instructions from the President of the United States, when you shall hear further from him.

I have the honor to be, with high respect, your obedient servant,

GEORGE CADWALADER,
Brevet Major-General U. S. A. Commanding.

The Chief Justice then inquired of the officer whether he had brought with him the body of John Merryman, and on being answered that he had no instructions but to deliver the return, the Chief Justice then said:

Gen. Cadwalader was commanded to produce the body of Mr. Merryman before me this morning, that the case might be heard, and the petitioner be either remanded to custody or set at liberty if held on insufficient grounds; but he has acted in disobedience to the writ, and I therefore direct that an attachment be at once issued against him, returnable before me here at twelve o'clock to-morrow. The order was then passed as follows:

Ordered, That an attachment forthwith issue against General George Cadwalader for a contempt in refusing to produce the body of John Merryman according to the command of the writ of habeas corpus returnable and returned before me to-day, and that said attachment be returned before me at 12 o'clock to-morrow, at the room of the Circuit Court.

R. B. TANEY.

Monday, *May 27th*, 1861.

The Clerk then issued the writ of attachment as directed.

At 12 o'clock on the 28th May, 1861, the Chief Justice again took his seat on the bench, and called for the Marshal's return to the writ of attachment. It was as follows:

I hereby certify to the Honorable Roger B. Taney, Chief Justice of the Supreme Court of the United States, that by virtue of the within writ of attachment to me directed on the 27th day of May, 1861, I proceeded on this 28th day of May, 1861, to Fort McHenry for the purpose of serving the said writ. I sent in my name at the outer gate—the messenger returned with the reply "that there was no answer to my card," and therefore could not serve the writ as I was commanded. I was not permitted to enter the gate. So answers

WASHINGTON BONIFANT,
U. S. Marshal for the District of Maryland.

After it was read, the Chief Justice said, that the Marshal had the power to summon the *posse comitatus* to aid him in seizing and bringing before the Court, the party named in the attachment, who would, when so brought in, be liable to punishment by fine and imprisonment. But where, as in this case, the power refusing obedience was so notoriously superior to any the Marshal could command, he held that officer excused from doing anything more than he had done. The Chief Justice then proceeded as follows :

"I ordered this attachment yesterday, because, upon the face of the return, the detention of the prisoner was unlawful, upon the grounds :

"First—That the President, under the Constitution of the United States, *cannot suspend the privilege of the writ of habeas corpus,* nor authorize a military officer to do it.

"Second—A military officer has no right to arrest and detain a person not subject to the rules and articles of war for an offence against the laws of the United States, except in aid of the judicial authority, and subject to its control ; and if the party is arrested by the military, it is the duty of the officer to deliver him over immediately to the civil authority to be dealt with according to law."

It is therefore very clear that John Merryman, the petitioner, is entitled to be set at liberty and discharged immediately from imprisonment.

"I forbore yesterday to state orally the provisions of the Constitution of the United States which make those principles the fundamental law of the Union, because an oral statement might be misunderstood in some portions of it, and I shall therefore put my opinion in writing, and file it in the office of the Clerk of the Circuit Court in the course of this week."

He concluded by saying that he should cause his opinion, when filed, and all the proceedings to be laid before the President, in order that he might perform his constitutional duty, to enforce the laws by securing obedience to the process of the United States.

OPINION.

EX PARTE

JOHN MERRYMAN.

{ *Before the Chief Justice of the Supreme Court of the United States, at Chambers.*

The application in this case for a writ of *habeas corpus* is made to me under the 14th section of the Judiciary Act of 1789, which renders effectual for the citizen the constitutional privilege of the writ of *habeas corpus.* That act gives to the Courts of the United States, as well as to each Justice of the Supreme Court, and to every District Judge, power to grant writs of *habeas corpus* for the purpose of an inquiry into the cause of commitment. The petition was presented to me at Washington under the impression that I would order the prisoner to be brought before me there, but as he was confined in Fort McHenry, at the city of Baltimore, which is in my circuit, I resolved to hear it in the latter city, as obedience to the writ, under such circumstances, would not withdraw General Cadwalader, who had him in charge, from the limits of his military command.

The petition presents the following case: The petitioner resides in Maryland, in Baltimore County. While peaceably in his own house, with his family, it was, at 2 o'clock, on the morning of the 25th of May, 1861, entered by an armed force, professing to act under military orders. He was then compelled to rise from his bed, taken into custody, and conveyed to Fort McHenry, where he is imprisoned by the commanding officer, without warrant from any lawful authority.

The Commander of the Fort, General George Cadwalader, by whom he is detained in confinement, in his return to the writ, does not deny any of the facts alleged in the petition. He states that the prisoner was arrested by order of General Keim, of Pennsylvania, and conducted as aforesaid to Fort McHenry by his order, and placed in his (General Cadwalader's) custody, to be there detained by him as a prisoner.

A copy of the warrant or order under which the prisoner was arrested was demanded by his counsel, and refused: And it is not alleged in the return that any specific act, constituting any offence against the laws of the United States, has been charged against him upon oath, but he appears to have been arrested upon general charges of treason and rebellion, without proof, and without giving the names of the witnesses, or specifying the acts which, in the judgment of the military officer, constituted these crimes. And having the prisoner thus in custody upon these vague and unsupported accusations, he refuses to obey the writ of *habeas corpus*, upon the ground that he is duly authorized by the President to suspend it.

The case, then, is simply this:—A military officer, residing in Pennsylvania, issues an order to arrest a citizen of Maryland, upon vague and indefinite charges, without any proof, so far as appears. Under this order, his house is entered in the night; he is seized as a prisoner, and conveyed to Fort McHenry, and there kept in close confinement. And when a *habeas corpus* is served on the commanding officer, requiring him to produce the prisoner before a Justice of the Supreme Court, in order that he may examine into the legality of the imprisonment, the answer of the officer is that he is authorized by the President to suspend the writ of *habeas corpus* at his discretion, and, in the exercise of that discretion, suspends it in this case, and on that ground refuses obedience to the writ.

As the case comes before me, therefore, I understand that the President not only claims the right to suspend

the writ of *habeas corpus* himself, at his discretion, but
to delegate that discretionary power to a military officer,
and to leave it to him to determine whether he will or
will not obey judicial process that may be served upon
him.

No official notice has been given to the courts of justice, or to the public, by proclamation or otherwise,
that the President claimed this power, and had exercised it in the manner stated in the return. And I certainly listened to it with some surprise, for I had supposed
it to be one of those points of constitutional law upon
which there was no difference of opinion, and that it
was admitted on all hands that the privilege of the writ
could not be suspended, except by act of Congress.

When the conspiracy of which Aaron Burr was the
head became so formidable, and was so extensively
ramified as to justify, in Mr. Jefferson's opinion, the suspension of the writ, he claimed, on his part, no power
to suspend it, but communicated his opinion to Congress, with all the proofs in his possession, in order that
Congress might exercise its discretion upon the subject,
and determine whether the public safety required it.
And in the debate which took place upon the subject,
no one suggested that Mr. Jefferson might exercise the
power himself if, in his opinion, the public safety demanded it.

Having, therefore, regarded the question as too plain
and too well settled to be open to dispute, if the commanding officer had stated that upon his own responsibility, and in the exercise of his own discretion, he refused obedience to the writ, I should have contented
myself with referring to the clause in the Constitution,
and to the construction it received from every jurist and
statesman of that day, when the case of Burr was before
them. But being thus officially notified that the privilege of the writ has been suspended under the orders,
and by the authority, of the President, and believing, as
I do, that the President has exercised a power which he
does not possess under the Constitution, a proper respect
for the high office he fills requires me to state plainly and
fully the grounds of my opinion, in order to show that I

have not ventured to question the legality of his act without a careful and deliberate examination of the whole subject.

The clause of the Constitution, which authorizes the suspension of the privilege of the writ of *habeas corpus*, is in the 9th section of the first article.

This article is devoted to the legislative department of the United States, and has not the slightest reference to the Executive department. It begins by providing "that all legislative powers therein granted shall be vested in a Congress of the United States, which shall consist of a Senate and House of Representatives." And after prescribing the manner in which these two branches of the legislative department shall be chosen, it proceeds to enumerate specifically the legislative powers which it thereby grants; and, at the conclusion of this specification, a clause is inserted giving Congress "the power to make all laws which may be necessary and proper for carrying into execution the foregoing powers, and all other powers vested by this Constitution in the Government of the United States or in any department or office thereof."

The power of legislation granted by this latter clause is by its words carefully confined to the specific objects before enumerated. But as this limitation was unavoidably somewhat indefinite, it was deemed necessary to guard more effectually certain great cardinal principles essential to the liberty of the citizen, and to the rights and equality of the States, by denying to Congress, in express terms, any power of legislation over them. It was apprehended, it seems, that such legislation might be attempted under the pretext that it was necessary and proper to carry into execution the powers granted; and it was determined that there should be no room to doubt, where rights of such vital importance were concerned, and accordingly, this clause is immediately followed by an enumeration of certain subjects, to which the powers of legislation shall not extend ; and the great importance which the framers of the Constitution attached to the privilege of the writ of *habeas corpus* to protect the liberty of the citizen is proved by the fact that its suspension, except in cases of invasion and rebellion, is first in the list of prohibited powers—and even in these cases the power is denied, and its exercise prohibited, unless the public safety shall require it.

It is true that in the cases mentioned, Congress is of necessity the judge of whether the public safety does or does not require it; and their judgment is conclusive. But the introduction of these words is a standing admonition to the legislative body of the danger of suspending it, and of the extreme caution they should exercise before they give the Government of the United States such power over the liberty of a citizen.

It is the second article of the Constitution that provides for the organization of the Executive Department, and enumerates the powers conferred on it, and prescribes its duties. And if the high power over the liberty of the citizen now claimed was intended to be conferred on the President, it would undoubtedly be found in plain words in this article. But there is not a word in it that can furnish the slightest ground to justify the exercise of the power.

The article begins by declaring that the Executive power shall be vested in a President of the United States of America, to hold his office during the term of four years—and then proceeds to prescribe the mode of election, and to specify in precise and plain words the powers delegated to him and the duties imposed upon him. And the short term for which he is elected, and the narrow limits to which his power is confined, show the jealousy and apprehensions of future danger which the framers of the Constitution felt in relation to that department of the Government, and how carefully they withheld from it many of the powers belonging to the Executive branch of the English Government which were considered as dangerous to the liberty of the subject—and conferred (and that in clear and specific terms) those powers only which were deemed essential to secure the successful operation of the Government.

He is elected, as I have already said, for the brief term of four years, and is made personally responsible, by impeachment, for malfeasance in office. He is from necessity and the nature of his duties the commander-in-chief of the army and navy, and of the militia, when called into actual service. But no appropriation for the support of the army can be made by Congress for a longer term than two years, so that it is in the power of the succeeding House of Representatives to withhold the appropriation for its support, and thus disband it, if, in their judgment, the President used, or designed to use it for improper purposes. And although the militia, when in actual service, are under his command, yet the appointment of the officers is reserved to the States as a security against the use of the military power for purposes dangerous to the liberties of the people or the rights of the States.

So, too, his powers in relation to the civil duties and authority necessarily conferred on him are carefullly restricted, as well as those belonging to his military character. He cannot appoint the ordinary officers of government, nor make a treaty with a foreign nation or Indian tribe, without the advice and consent of the Senate, and cannot appoint even inferior officers, unless he is authorized by an act of Congress to do so. He is not empowered to arrest any one charged with an offence against the United States and whom he may, from the evidence before him, believe to be guilty; nor can he authorize any officer, civil or military, to exercise this power, for the 5th article of the Amendments to the Constitution expressly provides that no person "shall be deprived of life, liberty or property, without due process of law"—that is, judicial process.

And even if the privilege of the writ of *habeas corpus* were suspended by act of Congress, and a party not sub· ject to the rules and articles of war was afterwards arrested and imprisoned by regular judicial process, he could not be detained in prison or brought to trial before a military tribunal, for the article in the Amendments to the Constitution immediately following the one above referred to—that is, the 6th article—provides that "In all criminal prosecutions the accused shall enjoy the right to a speedy and public trial by an impartial jury of the State and district wherein the crime shall have been committed, which district shall have been previously ascertained by law, and to be informed of the nature and cause of the accusation ; to be confronted with the witnesses against him ; to have compulsory process for obtaining witnesses in his favor, and to have the assistance of counsel for his defence."

And the only power, therefore, which the President possesses, where the "life, liberty or property" of a private citizen is concerned, is the power and duty prescribed in the third section of the second article, which requires "that he shall take care that the laws shall be faithfully executed." He is not authorized to execute them himself, or through agents or officers, civil or military, appointed by himself, but he is to take care that they be faithfully carried into execution, as they are expounded and adjudged by the co-ordinate branch of the Government to which that duty is assigned by the Constitution. It is thus made his duty to come in aid of the judicial authority, if it shall be resisted by a force too strong to be overcome without the assistance of the Executive arm. But in exercising this power he acts in subordination to judicial authority, assisting it to execute its process and enforce its judgments.

With such provisions in the Constitution, expressed in language too clear to be misunderstood by any one, I can see no ground whatever for supposing that the President, in any emergency or in any state of things, can authorize the suspension of the privileges of the writ of *habeas corpus*, or arrest a citizen, except in aid of the judicial power. He certainly does not faithfully execute the laws if he takes upon himself legislative power by suspending the writ of *habeas corpus*, and the judicial power also, by arresting and imprisoning a person without due process of law. Nor can any argument be drawn from the nature of sovereignty, or the necessity of government, for self-defence in times of tumult and danger. The Government of the United States is one of delegated and limited powers. It derives its existence and authority altogether from the Constitution, and neither of its branches, Executive, Legislative, or Judicial can exercise any of the powers of Government beyond those specified and granted.

For the 10th article of the Amendments to the Constitution in express terms provides that "the powers not delegated to the United States by the Constitution, nor prohibited by it to the States, are reserved to the States respectively, or to the people."

Indeed, the security against imprisonment by executive authority, provided for in the fifth article of the Amendments to the Constitution, which I have before quoted, is nothing more than a copy of a like provision in the English Constitution, which had been firmly established before the Declaration of Independence.

Blackstone, in his Commentaries (1st vol., 137) states it in the following words :

"To make imprisonment lawful, it must be either by process of law from the Courts of Judicature or by warrant from some legal officer having authority to commit to prison." And the people of the United Colonies, who had themselves lived under its protection while they were British subjects, were well aware of the necessity of this safeguard for their personal liberty. And no one can believe that in framing a government intended to guard still more efficiently the rights and liberties of the citizen against executive encroachment and oppression, they would have conferred on the President a power which the history of England had proved to be dangerous and oppressive in the hands of the Crown, and which the people of England had compelled it to surrender after a long and obstinate struggle on the part of the English Executive to usurp and retain it.

The right of the subject to the benefit of the writ of *habeas corpus*, it must be recollected, was one of the great points in controversy during the long struggle in England between arbitrary government and free institutions, and must therefore have strongly attracted the attention of the statesmen engaged in framing a new and, as they supposed, a freer government than the one which they had thrown off by the revolution. For from the earliest history of the common law, if a person were imprisoned, no matter by what authority, he had a right to the writ of *habeas corpus* to bring his case before the King's Bench ; and if no specific offence was charged against him in the warrant of commitment, he was entitled to be forthwith discharged; and if an offence was charged which was bailable in its character, the court was bound to set him at liberty on bail. And the most exciting contests between the Crown and the people of England from the time of Magna Charta were in relation to the privilege of this writ, and they continued until the passage of the statute of 31st Charles 2d, commonly known as the great *habeas corpus* act.

This statute put an end to the struggle, and finally and firmly secured the liberty of the subject against the usurpation and oppression of the Executive branch of the Government. It nevertheless conferred no new right upon the subject, but only secured a right already existing. For, although the right could not justly be denied, there was often no effectual remedy against its violation. Until the statute of 13th William 3d the Judges held their offices at the pleasure of the King, and the influence which he exercised over timid, timeserving, and partisan judges often induced them, upon some pretext or other, to refuse to discharge the party, although entitled by law to his discharge, or delayed their decisions from time to time, so as to prolong the imprisonment of persons who were obnoxious to the King for their political opinions, or had incurred his resentment in any other way.

The great and inestimable value of the *habeas corpus* act of the 31st Charles 2d is that it contains provisions which compel courts and judges, and all parties concerned, to perform their duties promptly, in the manner specified in the statute.

A passage in Blackstone's Commentaries, showing the ancient state of the law on this subject, and the abuses which were practised through the power and influence of the Crown, and a short extract from Hallam's Constitutional History, stating the circumstances which gave rise to the passage of this statute, explain briefly, but fully, all that is material to this subject.

Blackstone, in his Commentaries on the Laws of England (3d vol. 133, 134) says:

"To assert an absolute exemption from imprisonment in all cases is inconsistent with every idea of law and political society, and in the end would destroy all civil liberty by rendering its protection impossible.

"But the glory of the English law consists in clearly defining the times, the causes, and the extent, when, wherefore, and to what degree the imprisonment of the subject may be lawful. This it is which induces the abolute necessity of expressing upon every commitment the reason for which it is made, that the court upon a *habeas corpus* may examine into its validity, and according to the circumstances of the case may discharge, admit to bail or remand the prisoner.

"And yet early in the reign of Charles I. the Court of King's Bench, relying on some arbitrary precedents (and those perhaps misunderstood) determined that they would not, upon a *habeas corpus*, either bail or deliver a prisoner, though committed without any cause assigned, in case he was committed by the special command of the King or by the Lords of the Privy Council. This drew on a Parliamentary inquiry and produced the *Petition of Right*—3 Charles 1—which recites this illegal judgment, and enacts that no freeman hereafter shall be so imprisoned or detained. But when in the following year Mr. Selden and others were committed by the Lords of the Council in pursuance of his Majesty's special command, under a general charge of 'notable contempts, and stirring up sedition against the King and the Government,' the judges delayed for two terms (including also the long vacation) to deliver an opinion how far such a charge was bailable. And when at length they agreed that it was, they however annexed a condition of finding sureties for their good behavior, which still protracted their imprisonment, the Chief Justice, Sir Nicholas Hyde, at the same time declaring that 'if they were again remanded for that cause perhaps the Court would not afterward grant a *habeas corpus*, being already made acquainted with the cause of the imprisonment.' But this was heard with indignation and astonishment by every lawyer present, according to Mr. Selden's own account of the matter, whose resentment was not cooled at the distance of four and twenty years."

It is worthy of remark that the offences charged against the prisoner in this case, and relied on as a justification for his arrest and imprisonment, in their nature and character, and in the loose and vague manner in which they are stated, bear a striking resemblance to those assigned in the warrant for the arrest of Mr. Selden. And yet, even at that day, the warrant was regarded as such a flagrant violation of the rights of the subject that the delay of the time-serving judges to set him at liberty upon the *habeas corpus* issued in his behalf excited the universal indignation of the bar. The extract from Hallam's Constitutional History is equally impressive and equally in point. (It is in vol. 4: p. 9, and is also cited at length in the note to pp. 136, 137 of the 3d volume of Wendell's edition of Blackstone.)

"It is a very common mistake, and not only among foreigners, but many from whom some knowledge of our constitutional laws might be expected, to suppose that this statute of Charles II. enlarged in a great degree our liberties, and forms a sort of epoch in their history. But though a very beneficial enactment, and eminently remedial in many cases of illegal imprisonment, it introduced no new principle, nor conferred any right upon the subject. From the earliest records of the English law, no freeman could be detained in prison, except upon a criminal charge or conviction, or for a civil debt. In the former case it was always in his power to demand of the Court of King's Bench a writ of *habeas corpus ad subjiciendum* directed to the person detaining him in custody, by which he was enjoined to bring up the body of the prisoner with the warrant of commitment that the Court might judge of its sufficiency and remand the party, admit him to bail, or discharge him, according to the nature of the charge. This writ issued of right, and could not be refused by the Court. It was not to bestow an immunity from arbitrary imprisonment, which is abundantly provided for in Magna Charta, (if, indeed, it is not more ancient,) that the statute of Charles II. was enacted, but to cut off the abuses by which the Government's lust of power, and the servile subtlety of Crown lawyers, had impaired so fundamental a privilege."

While the value set upon this writ in England has been so great that the removal of the abuses which embarrassed its enjoyment have been looked upon as almost a new grant of liberty to the subject, it is not to be wondered at that the continuance of the writ thus made effective should have been the object of the most jealous care. Accordingly, no power in England short of that of Parliament can suspend or authorize the suspension of the writ of *habeas corpus.* I quote again from Blackstone (1 Comm., 136:) "But the happiness of our Constitution is that it is not left to the Executive power to determine when the danger of the State is so great as to render this measure expedient. It is the Parliament only or legislative power that whenever it sees proper, can authorize the Crown by suspending the *habeas corpus* for a short and limited time, to imprison suspected persons without giving any reason for so doing." And if the President of the United States may suspend the writ, then the Constitution of the United States has conferred upon him more regal and absolute power over the liberty of the citizen than the people of England have thought it safe to entrust to the Crown—a power which the Queen of England cannot exercise at this day, and which could not have been lawfully exercised by the sovereign even in the reign of Charles the First.

But I am not left to form my judgment upon this great question from analogies between the English Government and our own, or the commentaries of English jurists, or the decisions of English courts, although upon this subject they are entitled to the highest respect, and are justly regarded and received as authoritative by our courts of justice. To guide me to a right conclusion, I have the commentaries on the Constitution of the United States of the late Mr. Justice Story, not only one of the most eminent jurists of the age, but for a long time one of the brightest ornaments of the Supreme Court of the United States, and also the clear and authoritative decision of that Court itself, given more than half a century since, and conclusively establishing the principles I have above stated.

Mr. Justice Story, speaking in his Commentaries of the *habeas corpus* clause in the Constitution, says:

"It is obvious that cases of a peculiar emergency may arise which may justify, nay, even require, the temporary suspension of any right to the writ. But as it has frequently happened in foreign countries, and even in England, that the writ has, upon various pretexts and occasions, been suspended, whereby persons apprehended upon suspicion have suffered a long imprisonment, sometimes from design, and sometimes because they were forgotten, the right to suspend it is expressly confined to cases of rebellion or invasion, where the public safety may require it. A very just and wholesome restraint, which cuts down at a blow a fruitful means of oppression, capable of being abused in bad times to the worst of purposes. Hitherto no suspension of the writ has ever been authorized by Congress since the establishment of the constitution. It would seem, as the power is given to Congress to suspend the writ of *habeas corpus* in cases of rebellion or invasion, that the right to judge whether the exigency had arisen must exclusively belong to that body." 3 Story's Com. on the Constitution, section 1336.

And Chief Justice Marshall, in delivering the opinion of the Supreme Court in the case of *ex parte* Bollman and Swartwout, uses this decisive language in 4 Cranch, 95 : "It may be worthy of remark that this act (speaking of the one under which I am proceeding) was passed by the first Congress of the United States sitting under a Constitution which had declared 'that the privilege of the writ of *habeas corpus* should not be suspended, unless when in cases of rebellion or invasion, the public safety might require it.' Acting under the immediate influence of this injunction, they must have felt, with peculiar force, the obligation of providing efficient means by which this great constitutional privilege should receive life and activity ; for if the means be not in existence, the privilege itself would be lost, although no law for its suspension should be enacted. Under the impression of this obligation they give to all the Courts the power of awarding writs of *habeas corpus.*"

And again, in page 101 :

"If at any time the public safety should require the suspension of the powers vested by this act in the courts of the United States, it is for the Legislature to say so. That question depends on political considerations, on which the Legislature is to decide. Until the Legislative will be expressed, this court can only see its duty, and must obey the laws."

I can add nothing to these clear and emphatic words of my great predecessor.

But the documents before me, show that the military authority in this case has gone far beyond the mere suspension of the privilege of the writ of *habeas corpus*. It has, by force of arms, thrust aside the judicial authorities and officers to whom the Constitution has confided the power and duty of interpreting and administering the laws, and substituted a military government in its place, to be administered and executed by military officers. For at the time these proceedings were had against John Merryman, the District Judge of Maryland, the Commissioner appointed under the act of Congress, the District Attorney and the Marshal, all resided in the city of Baltimore, a few miles only from the home of the prisoner. Up to that time there had never been the slightest resistance or obstruction to the process of any court or judicial officer of the United States in Maryland, except by the military authority. And if a military officer, or any other person, had reason to believe that the prisoner had committed any offence against the laws of the United States, it was his duty to give information of the fact and the evidence to support it, to the District Attorney; and it would then have become the duty of that officer to bring the matter before the District Judge or Commissioner, and if there' was sufficient legal evidence to justify his arrest, the Judge or Commissioner would have issued his warrant to the Marshal to arrest him ; and upon the hearing of the case would have held him to bail, or committed him for trial, according to the character of the offence as it appeared in the testimony, or would have discharged him immediately, if there was not sufficient evidence to support the accusation.

There was no danger of any obstruction or resistance to the action of the civil authorities, and therefore no reason whatever for the interposition of the military.

And yet, under these circumstances a military officer, stationed in Pennsylvania, without giving any information to the District Attorney, and without any application to the judicial authorities, assumes to himself the judicial power in the District of Maryland; undertakes to decide what constitutes the crime of treason or rebellion; what evidence (if, indeed, he required any) is sufficient to support the accusation and justify the commitment; and commits the party, without a hearing even before himself, to close custody in a strongly garrisoned fort, to be there held, it would seem, during the pleasure of those who committed him.

The Constitution provides, as I have before said, that "no person shall be deprived of life, liberty or property, without due process of law." It declares that "the right of the people to be secure in their persons, houses, papers and effects, against unreasonable searches and seizures, shall not be violated, and no warrant shall issue, but upon probable cause, supported by oath or affirmation, and particularly describing the place to be searched, and the persons or things to be seized." It provides that the party accused shall be entitled to a speedy trial in a court of justice.

And these great and fundamental laws, which Congress itself could not suspend, have been disregarded and suspended, like the writ of *habeas corpus*, by a military order, supported by force of arms. Such is the case now before me, and I can only say that if the authority which the Constitution has confided to the judiciary department and judicial officers may thus upon any pretext or under any circumstances be usurped by the military power at its discretion, the people of the United States are no longer living under a government of laws, but every citizen holds life, liberty and property at the will and pleasure of the army officer in whose military district he may happen to be found.

In such a case my duty was too plain to be mistaken. I have exercised all the power which the Constitution

and laws confer upon me, but that power has been resisted by a force too strong for me to overcome. It is possible that the officer who has incurred this grave responsibility may have misunderstood his instructions, and exceeded the authority intended to be given him. I shall, therefore, order all the proceedings in this case. with my opinion, to be filed and recorded in the Circuit Court of the United States for the District of Maryland, and direct the Clerk to transmit a copy, under seal, to the President of the United States. It will then remain for that high officer, in fulfilment of his constitutional obligation to "take care that the laws be faithfully executed," to determine what measures he will take to cause the civil process of the United States to be respected and enforced.   R. B. TANEY,
Chief Justice of the Supreme Court United States.

www.ingramcontent.com/pod-product-compliance
Lightning Source LLC
Chambersburg PA
CBHW020707260626
47157CB00008B/3179